THE SECRETS OF DROON

Dream Thief

by Tony Abbott

Illustrated by David Merrell

Cover illustration by Tim Jessell

A
LITTLE APPLE
PAPERBACK

SCHOLASTIC INC.
New York Toronto London Auckland Sydney
Mexico City New Delhi Hong Kong Buenos Aires

For all who dream,
may your adventures never end

For more information about the continuing saga of Droon,
please visit Tony Abbott's website at
www.tonyabbottbooks.com

Book design by Dawn Adelman

No part of this publication may be reproduced in whole or in part,
or stored in a retrieval system, or transmitted in any form or by any means,
electronic, mechanical, photocopying, recording, or otherwise,
without written permission of the publisher.
For information regarding permission, write to Scholastic Inc.,
Attention: Permissions Department, 557 Broadway, New York, NY 10012.

ISBN 0-439-42078-4

12 11 10 9 8 7   4 5 6 7 8/0

Printed in the U.S.A.   40
First printing, February 2003

Contents

One

Droon Dreams

Clank! Plong! Eric Hinkle swung his curved fighting stick at the five-headed, seven-armed beast in the nasty dark dungeon.

"*Grrrroooo!*" the creature snarled. In six huge hands it swung six giant clubs. In the seventh hand, it held . . . Princess Keeah!

"Help!" she screamed. "Save me, Eric!"

"Don't worry. I'll take care of this!" said Eric calmly. With one swift jerk of his stick,

* 1 *

he forced the beast back and pulled Keeah to safety.

"My hero!" she cried.

"Thanks, but we're not out of the castle yet." Taking off at a run, Eric whisked Keeah through a series of dark hallways, leaped across a burning bridge, and swung on a chain across a pit of serpents.

"The gate is bolted!" cried Keeah, her golden hair flying as they raced to escape.

"No problem," he said. "Watch this —"

Even jumping down stairs three at a time, with the princess on his arm, Eric sent a perfect stream of blue sparks from his fingertips.

Zzzing! The gate flew apart, and they were suddenly free, outside under a pink sky with wispy purple clouds. All around them crowds of people were calling out, "Hooray, Eric! You did it. Three cheers for the greatest hero ever!"

And *that* was the moment when something in Eric's mind reminded him that he was sleeping.

"It's a dream," he mumbled to himself, turning over on his side. "It's only a dream. . . ."

It *was* a dream. Eric knew he was at home in his bed, fast asleep. But he also knew where he was in the dream. It could only be one place.

The land of Droon.

Droon was the mysterious and secret world he and his friends Neal and Julie had discovered one day under his basement stairs.

It was a land of enchantment and awesome adventure. It was filled with strange places and creatures — some good, others not so good.

Right now, Eric was dreaming about one of the good ones.

"You saved me, Eric. Thank you," said Keeah, smiling at him. She was one of his best friends in Droon and a young wizard herself.

In the crowd nearby were Keeah's parents, Queen Relna and King Zello. Next to them stood Galen, the greatest of all wizards, his white beard trailing to his waist, his old hands waving to Eric.

"Cool!" Eric said to himself, searching the crowd. "Everybody came. Well, not everybody. I'm glad stinky old Sparr isn't here!"

Lord Sparr was the wicked ruler of Droon's Dark Lands and an evil sorcerer of great power.

Sparr was in the Upper World now — Eric's world — lost sometime in the last five hundred years. A sorceress named Salamandra had taken his place in Droon.

Jabbo, a plump little dragon who baked pies for her, had come to Droon, too.

"Hooray for Eric the wizard!" people shouted.

Eric smiled at that. Ever since a blast of Keeah's magic zapped him, his finger-tips sparked with blue light, and he could see visions of things that hadn't happened yet.

"Yoo-hoo, Eric! You go, dear!"

"Huh?" He turned, surprised to see his mother cheering from the crowd. His father was there, too, and even his grandparents.

"Cool dream," he said, waving back.

Whoosh! A golden door opened in front of Eric, and he entered a room filled with light.

From the light came a voice. *Eric . . . enter!*

It was a woman's voice, soft and musi

cal. It spoke in a whisper . . . far away . . . and quiet.

Eric, come in. You are . . . one of us!

He had heard those words before. Lord Sparr had once said to Galen that Eric was "one of us." Since then, the kids had learned that Galen had two brothers. One of them was Urik, a great wizard and wandmaker.

The other was Sparr himself.

All three were the sons of a good and powerful wizard queen named Zara. Long ago, Zara had been kidnapped from the Upper World and brought to Droon.

Strangely, it always gave Eric a mysterious ache to speak her name.

But how Eric was "one of them," no one knew.

Now, as he neared the light, it seemed as if a hand, thin and white, was reaching out to him.

Take the gift!

Eric opened his own hand. "A prize? For me?"

The one who strikes the wolf at noon, shall earn a secret wish in Droon. . . .

"You mean me? Is it noon now? What secret wish? Excuse me, but who exactly are you?"

But the voice was suddenly muffled, and the great golden hall around him began to fade.

"Wait! My prize, my dream!" Eric felt himself falling backward away from the hand. "Hey!"

All of a sudden — *kkkk-foom!* — the light flashed and went out completely. The hand was gone, the light was gone, the room was gone.

The air around him now smelled damp,

and there was water . . . *drip* . . . *drip* . . . *dripping* . . . somewhere behind him.

"Um, I think I liked my first dream better."

He was in a room made of strange, silvery stone, lit by a sort of smoky light from above. And there, huddled in a shaft of that light, was a dragon.

But it was not the usual sort of dragon. This one was short and chubby and wore an apron smudged with purple and red stains.

Fruit stains.

Eric blinked. "Jabbo? . . . The pie maker?"

It was Jabbo, the strange little dragon who baked pies for the wicked Princess Salamandra.

"What are you doing in my dream?" asked Eric. "It was going so well, too. I was a big hero. I was going to get a prize —"

But Jabbo wasn't paying any attention.

The dragon was murmuring softly to himself. "Well, now, look at this. Jabbo stares at the thing . . . and it stares right back!"

Eric edged into the smoky light. "What do you have there? What's staring back at you?"

Jabbo held up a small shiny object.

A blue flame seemed to flicker deep inside it.

Eric gasped. He had seen the object before.

It was a small gem called the Eye of the Viper. It was one of two identical gems that belonged to Lord Sparr. Jabbo had gotten hold of one just before he escaped from the Upper World into Droon.

The dragon suddenly stood up. "Jabbo has decided. He doesn't want to bake pies anymore! Not when he can have such . . . power! With this pretty jewel, Jabbo can rule over Droon!"

Eric drew in a short breath. "Wait, no. Jabbo, I think that jewel is way too powerful for you. Too powerful for any of us. It can make your mind go a little nutty. Especially if Sparr still has the other one!"

Eric had had the jewel for a short time himself, and it had played tricks with his mind. "I think we need to give it to Galen —"

"These words," said Jabbo, holding the gem to the gray light. "I wonder what they mean."

"Jabbo, let's go find a nice kitchen for you to bake some pies in —"

"*Cha-go . . . Hakoth-Mal . . . kala-na-drem . . . esh-kee-tah. . . .*"

"Okay," said Eric. "Stop with the baby talk and give me the jewel —"

Jabbo made a sudden gasping noise. Trembling, he pointed behind Eric.

Eric's blood turned cold. "Uh . . . I'm

not going to like what I see when I turn around, am I?"

Jabbo shook his head. "I don't think so."

"Man, I really liked my first dream better —"

There was a sudden fluttering sound from the shadows — *flit-t-t-t!*

"Wh-wh-wh-who's there?" asked Eric, turning.

He gasped when he saw it. It was a warrior in rust-red armor, standing upright like a man, but with the head of a wolf. Growing from its back were two black wings.

"Correction," said Eric. "You're not a who. You're a *what!* And what exactly *are* you?"

"He came from the jewel!" said Jabbo, suddenly delighted. "See! With the gem, Jabbo commands great warriors!"

"Uh-huh, well, command him to go away."

"Jabbo doesn't know the words for that."

"Try more baby talk!" said Eric.

Klish-ang! Gleaming claws shot out from the creature's hands. The beast flashed them across the air — *shwee-shwee!*

Eric backed up. "Okay, put those things away before someone gets hurt. Someone like me!"

Fwip! Its wings flicked once, and the armored creature sprang across the floor.

"Come on now!" Eric cried, glancing around for a place to hide, but finding none. "It's only a dream, right? I'm asleep. I'm dreaming. I can't get hurt in a dream, can I? Can I?"

Fwip! The creature sprang closer.

It raised its terrible claws.

Eric buried his head in his arms. "Nooooooo!"

Shwee! Shwee!

Two

Wake-up Call

"Nooooooo!" Eric was still screaming when a hand suddenly grabbed his shoulder.

"Hey, pal, wake up. It's me —"

Eric pulled his face from his hands and his eyes popped open. He found himself staring into the smiling face of his best friend Neal.

"Huh? What? Neal? Where am I?"

"In your bed, dreaming," said his friend

* 14 *

with a grin. "And from the silly noises you were making, it sounded like a bad one."

Eric blinked. The room was gray. "But it's so early. What are you doing here?"

"I had a weird Droon dream and rushed right over," he said. "Your folks let us in."

"Us?" asked Eric.

"I'm here, too," said the voice of his other best friend, Julie, stepping into the room.

Eric sat up in bed. The birds were chirping noisily outside. It was clearly morning.

"You had dreams, too?" asked Eric. "Tell me."

"Mine started out the absolute coolest," said Julie. "I was training pilkas on this beautiful white beach in Droon, when — boom! Jabbo is there. Only he's not into making pies anymore. He's talking about taking over!"

"Jabbo busted up my dream, too," said

Neal. "I was just about to split a huge gizzleberry cake with Max — it was big! — when Jabbo stomps the cake to mush. He said it was undercooked!"

Eric stared at his friends. "This is so incredible. Jabbo interrupted my dream, too. I was busy rescuing Keeah from a monster. Crowds were cheering all over the place. It seemed so real. Then a voice starts speaking to me —"

"A voice? What did it say?" asked Julie.

"Something about the stuff I need to do in Droon —"

"That sounds fairly important," said Neal. "All I was trying to do was eat a cake."

"But that all vanished when Jabbo appeared," Eric went on. "He had the Eye of the Viper. He spoke some weird words and the next thing I know this crazy wolf dude is coming after me. Luckily, you woke me up."

Julie chuckled. "Eric, you can't get hurt in your dreams. At least, I don't think you can."

"Well, it seemed pretty real," said Eric. "In the first part I was getting a prize for saving Keeah."

"A prize?" Julie laughed. "Is that what you have in your hand?"

"Huh?" Eric held up his hand. It was clenched tightly in a fist. He opened it and gasped.

There, sitting in his palm, was a smooth round stone. Even in the dim room, it shone like silver.

Eric nearly fell out of bed. "Whoa! Where did this . . . I mean, how did I . . . I mean . . . whoa! This is the coolest, most amazing thing ever!"

Neal's eyes bugged out. "No wonder your dream seemed real. You even got a souvenir!"

"It looks magical," said Julie. "Does it have special powers now that you're a wizard?"

"I don't know." Eric turned the stone over and saw for the first time that there was a symbol carved into the stone. He had seen that symbol once before. It was from the old Droon language.

It was his name.

"Okay, this is important," said Julie, throwing up the shade and letting the morning light into the room. "Jabbo took over each of our dreams. Eric, you even woke up with stuff. Dreams are one of the ways we know to go to Droon. I think someone is telling us to get to Droon right away."

"Someone," said Eric, remembering the strange, faraway voice in his dream. "But who?"

Neal smiled. "Maybe we'll find out. Let's roll!"

While Neal and Julie waited in the hall, Eric scrambled into his clothes. He looked again at the silvery stone, then smiled to himself, remembering the crowds cheering for him. "Me. A hero. Cool." He slipped the stone into his pocket.

Two minutes later, the three friends bounded down to the kitchen, where Mr. Hinkle was mixing batter in a big bowl.

"Hey, kids," he said, "just in time for waffles!"

Neal sniffed deeply, then sighed. "Sorry, Mr. H. You know I'm always ready to put in my order, even when I'm not hungry, but we have to go downstairs for a sec."

That was one of the great things about going to Droon. No matter how long the kids were there, no time went by in the Upper World.

Mrs. Hinkle blinked. "Neal passing up breakfast? We must be dreaming!"

Eric laughed. "Something like that, Mom."

He wished he could stop and tell his parents how cool it was to see them in his dream. How special they were. But he wasn't sure the words would come out right. Plus, Droon was a secret.

Besides, Julie was already tugging him to the basement door. "Come on. Time is wasting."

"Be right back!" Eric yelled over his shoulder as his friends hustled him down to the basement. Together they pulled aside the boxes that hid a small closet under the stairs. Neal opened the door and switched on the light.

Eric patted the stone in his pocket. "I think I was about to learn something very important in my dream. I sort of feel as if I've been robbed."

"And Jabbo did the robbing," said Julie.

"He robbed all of us of some very cool dreams. Keeah and Galen need to know. Pronto."

"Plus, I never even got a bite of that cake," said Neal. "Talk about nightmares!"

With a laugh, everyone piled into the small room. Eric closed the door behind them. Julie turned off the light.

Click. The room went dark.

A moment later — *whoosh!* — the gray floor vanished beneath them. In its place stood the top step of a shimmering staircase. It spiraled down and away from the house.

Neal grinned. "Other people just have dirt and rocks under their houses, Eric. I hope you know how lucky you are."

Eric's heart raced. "Believe me, I know."

Step by step, the three friends descended the stairs, passing into a layer of wispy purple clouds. Eric remembered the clouds from his dream.

"Maybe it'll come true," he whispered.

Farther down, a fine pink mist surrounded them. The air was fresh and cool.

"It smells like morning," said Julie.

When they neared the bottom, a gentle breeze wafted over them, clearing the mist. Before them lay a hill of high grass waving in the breeze. Behind was a range of white cliffs and a sparkling blue sea. They stepped onto the ground.

As always, the staircase faded. It would return when it was time to leave Droon.

"Nice view from up here," said Eric, looking out over the cliffs.

"Um . . . not so nice from this angle," said Neal, backing up into Eric and Julie.

They turned. The tall grass in front of them was moving, but not back and forth in the breeze anymore. The grass was moving toward them.

Ssssss! it hissed.

"That grass is not grass," said Neal, trembling. "It's snakes! Millions of them. I don't like snakes!"

"But they're so cute," said Julie. "Maybe they're friendly —"

Whoomf! A short burst of green fire shot from the mouth of each snake.

"Fire-breathing snakes are not cute," said Neal. "Or friendly!"

With every wiggle toward the children, the snakes hissed, breathed out a puff of sharp green flame, and chanted a single word.

"Jabbo!"

Three

The Cave in the Cliff

Sssss! "Jabbo!" *Sssss!*

"You don't suppose this is how snakes say hello in Droon, do you?" asked Julie, backing up.

Neal shook his head. "No. I'm pretty sure this is how they say good-bye. They're pushing us toward the cliffs!"

Eric quickly raised his hands as they scrambled to the edge of the cliff. "Don't worry. I'll take care of this."

"Yeah, blast them!" said Neal. "You're the wizard hero and all that!"

"But don't hurt them," said Julie. "They're still kind of cute. Deadly, maybe, but still cute!"

"*Caro-baro-moo!*" said Eric, using words that popped into his head.

Zzzzt! A bolt of blue light shot from his fingertips and blasted the ground at their feet.

"Yikes!" cried Eric. "My aim was lots better in my dream!"

Just as the snakes gathered for another charge — *zzz-whoosh!* — a white mist streaked over them.

The snakes raised their tiny heads into the mist. "Jabbo?" they said. Then they plopped to the ground in little heaps and fell asleep — *snzz.*

The kids looked down. Their feet were teetering on the very edge of the cliff.

"That was really close!" said Neal.

"That was really me!" said a voice at their side. The kids looked over to see a spiral of blue light sparking and fizzing in the air. The light faded and out popped Princess Keeah herself. Her golden crown glinted in the sun, and her fingers still sizzled with white sparks.

Next to her was Max, the pug-nosed, orange-haired, eight-legged spider troll.

"Keeah! Are we glad to see you!" said Julie.

"Yeah," said Neal. "Another minute and we would have been snake snacks!"

The princess gave her friends a hug. "We were on our way to find Galen and join my parents' hunt for Salamandra when we saw you getting attacked."

Max stooped to the snoozing green pile. "Trouble with meadow snakes? This is new. With Sparr lost in the Upper

World, I thought Droon would have some peace."

"Not if Jabbo can help it," said Eric. "The snakes were chanting his name. If my dream is right, he's using the Eye of the Viper."

Keeah shot a serious look at Max, then turned to the kids. "Jabbo has appeared in our dreams, too. It started two nights ago."

Max shuddered, his bright orange hair standing straight up. "I'm afraid to sleep. Everyone's upset about the scary dreams."

"We'd better find Galen," said Keeah.

"Can we travel with that light spiral you used to get here?" asked Julie.

"No need!" said Max, pointing over the edge of the cliffs. "Galen's right down here. In his secret cave!"

With Keeah in the lead, the little band clambered over the edge and down the rocks to a small opening cut into the face of the cliff.

In the center of the cave, surrounded by books, maps, and several strange scientific instruments, was Galen himself.

He sat perched on a stool, his eyes clamped shut, singing in a scratchy old voice.

O, come to me, my Faraway!
Your voice as soft as feathers seems,
Come share your wisdom night and day
In wondrous visions and in dreams.

He stopped singing, but did not move from the stool.

"Ahem, master?" whispered Max.

Galen's finger shot up. "A moment, please!"

They waited for several seconds before the wizard's eyes popped open.

"Nothing!" he snorted. "I'm sorry, but I often get visions from someone I call the Faraway. It is only a dream voice, really. But I haven't dreamed lately. Not good dreams, at least. Ah, well . . ."

"That's exactly like the voice I heard," said Eric. "Faraway, but close, too, right? At least, I heard it until Jabbo started using the blue jewel he stole."

Galen bolted up from the stool. "So, you dream of Jabbo, too? That little pie maker is everywhere. Quickly now, tell me your dreams!"

One by one, Neal, Julie, and Eric told him the dreams that had woken them that morning.

"But that's not the really amazing part," said Neal. "Go on, Eric. Show them what you got."

Eric slid his hand into his pocket and

pulled out the silver stone. "My dream was more real than any I've ever had. I woke up with this."

The stone glistened in the sunlight.

Keeah's eyes widened. "It's beautiful."

"I once woke up with a peanut butter sandwich!" said Neal.

Julie laughed. "You fell asleep with it, too."

Galen chuckled, even as he took Eric's stone and examined it. "Max, please find out what you can about such stones."

"Yes, master!" chirped the spider troll. He scampered to a tall stack of books.

"Now, Eric," said Galen, "can you remember the words Jabbo spoke?"

"I think so." While Eric recited the words, Keeah wrote them, and Galen stroked his beard.

At last, the wizard spoke. "The words

date back to the earliest days of Goll. They mean, 'Go, Hakoth-Mal, hunt my enemies. Our day is coming.'"

Eric shivered. *Our day is coming.* Those were the same words Sparr had spoken to him when they last met. They didn't sound good then. They sounded even worse now.

The wizard sighed. "The warrior you saw in your dream, Eric, is part of a tribe of ancient hunters known as the Hakoth-Mal."

"The ha-ha what?" asked Neal.

"The Hakoth-Mal," said Galen. "I wish they were a laughing matter, but they are not. It is an old Droon word meaning wingwolves. They hunt down the enemies of their ruler."

"If their ruler is Sparr, then they're hunting us," said Keeah. "We have to be on our guard."

"I think so, yes." Galen strode to the cave opening and looked out over the sea. "Before the dreams stopped, the Faraway told me that this Coiled Viper of Sparr's is the third of his Three Powers, and perhaps the most dangerous of all." He frowned. "Sparr . . . my brother . . ."

The kids looked at one another. It was the first time Galen had called Sparr his brother.

"Sadly, I know nothing of what the Viper does," Galen went on, "but if a simple gem from it can cause so much trouble, we must fear it. Eric, your dream has told us much. It was a good thing."

Eric frowned. "It nearly scared me to death!"

"I'm pretty sure you can't get hurt in dreams," said Keeah. "At least, I hope not —"

Max suddenly gasped. "Uh-oh . . ."

"What is it?" asked Julie.

"As I feared," the spider troll said, tapping a small purple book. "The kind of silver stone Eric has is found only in the Dark Lands of Lord Sparr."

The children shivered to hear the words.

Eric took the stone and gazed at it closely. "Why would a stone with my name on it come from the Dark Lands? Is that where Jabbo is, too?"

Hrrrr! Hrrrr! At that moment, a strange whinnying sound echoed in the cave.

Keeah turned to Galen. "It sounds like a pilka. Someone is coming."

"Let's go up!" said Max.

Rushing back to the cliff top, they saw four pilkas galloping hard toward the cliff. The shaggy six-legged beasts were hitched to a chariot driven by a tall green-furred creature.

Keeah jumped. "Is that . . . yes! It's Or-tha!"

Ortha was queen of the monkeys who lived in the mysterious Bangledorn Forest. The children had met her once before.

Hrrrr! The pilkas galloped over and stopped.

Ortha leaped from the chariot. She was very tall and slender. Her green fur was the color of spring grass. Around her neck was a blue cape, and on her head a crown of purple leaves.

She looked worried, but her expression softened when she saw the children. "It is so good to see you again. I wish it were a happier time."

"Ortha, what brings you so far from your forest?" asked Galen.

"You know Bangledorn Forest as a calm, friendly place," she said. "But two days ago, birds came with stories of burn-

ing trees in the east. Last night, a fight began among the ground animals, all growling out a strange word I'd never heard before —"

"Let me guess," said Neal. "Jabbo?"

"Yes!" said Ortha. "Our forest has always been a place of peace. Now it is a place of nightmares."

Keeah, Eric, and the others told Ortha about the little dragon, while Galen unrolled a map of Droon and spread it on the ground. Running one finger along the boundary of ancient Goll and another around the forest, his fingers met.

"I see it now," he said finally. "One small part of your forest crosses into the Dark Lands. If Jabbo is making trouble in the forest, then *that* is where we shall find him."

He then turned to Eric, a smile creeping over his lips. "And perhaps the mystery of your silvery stone will be solved there, too. Yes, this excites me like the old days! Keeah, I think Salamandra can wait. In the meantime, I will send your parents a friend. Behold!"

The wizard opened his fist and, with a brief sizzling sound, something light and swift left his hand, fluttered up, and spun around the group.

"What is it?" asked Julie. "It's beautiful!"

"This is Flink, my friendly messenger. Flink, go to our king and queen. When they need me, come, and I will return with you."

"Yesssss, Galennn!" Flink's voice was like music as the creature spun around their heads. A moment later, it shot low over the waves and out to sea.

"That may be your last bit of magic, for a time," said Ortha. "Where we are going, there is no magic."

The kids knew what Ortha meant.

Bangledorn Forest was one of the few places in Droon where no magic was allowed.

"Come on, everybody," said Keeah. "We have a pie maker with a sorcerer's power. The longer we wait, the more trouble Jabbo can do."

With a gentle motion of the reins, Ortha turned the chariot to face the rising sun.

The small troop piled in and set off quickly for the great forest empire of the Bangledorn monkeys.

Four

Trouble in Paradise

For two hours the pilkas thundered across the plains. When the sun was nearly overhead, Ortha began to slow the chariot.

Before them stood a vast wall of trees. In the middle were two giant oaks whose upper branches arched and met to form a gate into the forest.

"It's magnificent," said Keeah.

"Bangledorn Forest is the most ancient

area of all," said Galen. "How long it has weathered the storms of Droon!"

"Let us hope it continues to," said Ortha grimly.

As the pilkas trotted under the arch, fat green leaves flicked and fluttered, and warm breezes swept through the trees. Vines dangled from above like long strands of brown and green hair.

And high overhead, through a canopy of lush leaves, was the sparkling light of the sun.

"It's like a wild jungle in here," said Neal, looking all around. "*So* cool."

Ortha smiled. "Nature is everything to the Bangledorns. Even though magic is not allowed here, we find magic wherever we look. Behold!"

As the chariot drove in, they looked up to see tree houses everywhere. Some had many levels among the branches. Others were small, with neat thatched roofs and flowers growing in front.

"Bangledorn City," said Galen, his eyes wide with wonder. "It makes my heart sing to see it again."

In the center of this big treetop city was the most gigantic tree house ever.

"Ortha's palace!" said Max. "There is no grander home in all of Droon!"

The queen's palace had many levels leading to a main hall that stood open to the air on all sides. Its roof was held up, not by walls, but by the branches of giant trees.

"My ancestors built Bangledorn City," said Ortha, "because of a dream they had of a place of peace, far from the struggles of Droon —"

Clack! Crash! Blamk! Flidd! The sounds of crashing sticks came from high above them.

"I think that peace is under attack," said Eric. "It sounds like fighting —"

"Now we see what Jabbo's scary dreams have done," said Max. "Look up there!"

In the high trees near the palace, one group of little green monkeys was throwing nuts at a second group in the palace's main hall.

"In my home, of all places!" said Ortha.

"Children, Max," said Galen, "you go up one tree. Ortha, you and I shall go up the other!"

In a flash, the children scrambled up a long vine ladder that led to the queen's palace. Reaching the main hall first, they stopped. The large room was empty.

"The monkeys were just here," said Julie.

"Wait," said Eric, tilting his head.

Thump . . . thump . . . Soft padding noises were coming from above them.

Keeah grinned. "The monkeys are on the roof! Let's go!" Quickly, she led them up a narrow set of steps and peered over the roof's edge.

One group of furry green monkeys, whose leader wore a purple scarf around his head, was carefully making its way across the thatched roof. They carried thick, curved sticks.

Two trees away was a second group, led by a tiny monkey wearing a red sash. They were armed with large brown nuts.

All of a sudden, the second group pierced the air with wild shrieks, leaped onto the roof, and began hurling nuts at the first group.

Bamph! Clonk! Thud!

"I am Jabbo, and I say, we fight you!" the red-sashed monkey cried.

"What?" cried the purple-scarfed leader.

"Everyone knows I am the true Jabbo! We'll beat you!"

The first group threw their sticks at the others.

"Nuts versus sticks?" said Neal.

"And Jabbo versus Jabbo!" said Julie.

"This is bad," said Eric. "Let's get the leaders down to the main hall. Ortha and Galen should be there by now."

"Good idea," said Keeah. "Come on. But no magic, remember."

Eric nodded. "I'll put my powers on standby."

The children climbed onto the roof.

"Ready . . . now!" said Keeah. The kids rushed the monkeys. Most of them scurried off into the trees. But the two leaders tried to escape through the palace's main hall — where Ortha was waiting for them.

"Got you!" she said, reaching out her

long arms and catching both of them. "Now then! What is the meaning of this?"

"Woot started it!" said the purple-scarfed one in a high voice, pointing to the red-sashed monkey. "She threw a big brown nut at me."

"Because he waved that stick!" said the other, in an even higher voice.

"Enough!" said Ortha, glaring at the two monkeys. "Twee and Woot! Brother and sister! How disgraceful! You two have dishonored my house and yourselves! What really started this? . . . Twee?"

The monkey named Twee hung his head. "My dreams went all dark and scary. Then I saw the dragon, Jabbo. I can be powerful and take over, too, just like him."

"And Woot?" said Ortha, frowning darkly.

"I didn't dream any nice dreams at all last night," Woot said, beginning to sniffle.

"Jabbo was in my head. Big feet clomping all around. It made me sad, then mad, then . . . bad!"

The two monkeys bowed before the queen.

"We are so sorry," said Woot.

"We truly are!" squeaked Twee.

Ortha's stern face softened. "Well, I can see that you are. And perhaps the best way to keep the peace is . . . to bring you with us!"

"A journey?" asked Twee.

"With our queen?" asked Woot.

Ortha nodded. "We are going to find Jabbo, and stop him from disturbing and *stealing* your good dreams."

"Besides, there are better things to do with sticks and big nuts," said Neal. "A little game called baseball is *way* more fun than fighting."

"Teach us! Teach us!" Twee and Woot cheered together.

Galen laughed. "Later. But tell us now, where was Jabbo when you saw him in your dreams?"

Woot blinked at Twee. "The temple?"

Twee nodded. "Yes! The big lost temple!"

Ortha shook her head. "Stories tell of an old temple of silver stone deep in the forest, but if it ever existed, it has been swallowed up by time."

"Silver stone?" asked Eric. "Like this?" He pulled the dream stone from his pocket.

"Just like that!" said Woot.

"I see, then," said Galen. "There is no doubt now about where we must go."

"The Dark Lands?" asked Keeah.

"The Dark Lands," he said. "Are we ready?"

"Almost!" Twee scampered over to a barrel on the palace deck and began shoving golden squares into the pockets of his belt.

Neal froze. "Wait. Is that . . . food?"

Woot's large blue eyes lit up. "Bangle-dorn monkey biscuits. Made fresh daily. Try some!"

Julie laughed. "If you let him, he'll try *all* of them!"

Neal grinned and filled his own pockets with the golden biscuits. "*Now* we're ready."

Keeah cheered. "Then — we're off!"

Five

Over the Sea of Trees

Ortha gathered the travelers on the high deck of her palace overlooking the city. "The way to the Dark Lands is east," she said. "And the only way to travel swiftly is to take the vine roads."

"The vine roads?" asked Max. "What are they?"

Twee and Woot laughed merrily. "Keeah knows! But we'll show you! Fol low us — up!"

The twin monkeys scampered up a winding staircase from the palace to the top of a high tree. Ortha, Galen, and Max followed closely, with the children bringing up the rear.

When they reached the top, they stopped, amazed by what they saw.

Bright sunlight shone down upon a glittering sea of green treetops. And stretching away as far as the eye could see were bridges — bridges made of vines and branches, looping and dipping from one treetop to the next.

"This is amazing!" said Julie, as the leaves quivered in the warm breeze. "It's like nothing I've ever seen before. Keeah, you knew about this?"

Keeah laughed. "Last year, I came to camp here to learn to control my powers. I spent lots of time in the high trees. I almost didn't want to come down."

"A camp to learn to control your powers?" said Eric. "I think that's what I need."

"We could do this back home," said Neal. "If we hung rope bridges from my backyard to your backyard, then over to Julie's house, we'd never have to touch the ground again!"

With a musical shout — "*O — lee — lee! O — lee — lee!*" — Ortha began the long journey.

The first bridge dipped between two of the very highest trees in the forest. From there, the roads twisted and turned, including many offshoots down to lower trees, houses, and even small villages built among the branches.

All day they traveled. The farther they went, the fewer animals they saw. The birds weren't chirping or cawing, and only a few monkeys played in the high branches.

"Jabbo's been stealing dreams here, too," said Keeah. "I can tell that the animals are upset."

"We monkeys live for our dreams," said Twee.

"My brother and I agree on that," said Woot. "We all feel lost and unhappy without nice dreams at night."

"Me, too," said Neal. "And if I have a nightmare, I wake up scared, too."

"Galen and Ortha are also worried about the dreams," said Julie.

The wizard walked the bridges, gazing into the misty distance or studying his map. Ortha was close behind, her tall frame bending to his.

"I bet it has something to do with that creepy wolf warrior Jabbo made appear," said Eric. "I keep feeling like I'm going to see him any minute."

But more than that, Eric wondered

what his stone had to do with Jabbo, or the "lost" temple, or dreams, or the Dark Lands. Was it really a prize for him? Or did it mean something else? Could it be *magical,* as Julie wondered?

By the time the sun began to set, the small group had traveled many miles.

"Our journey is a long one," said Galen, stopping to look at the darkening sky. "We'll sleep here and begin again when first light comes."

While Ortha and Max strung up vine hammocks under a large leafy canopy, Twee and Woot scampered into the trees and came back with fruits and nuts enough for a meal.

While they ate, Neal explained the rules of baseball until nearly everyone curled up, exhausted.

"I guess we'd better sleep, too," said Keeah, turning over in her hammock.

So did Julie. Then Neal. Finally, even Galen, Max, and Ortha went quiet.

Eric breathed in the night air. The forest was dark and hushed. But it wasn't peaceful.

"That Hakoth-Mal is out there," he whispered to himself. He patted his pocket and remembered the soft voice from his dream. Would he be the one to strike the wolf at noon and earn a secret wish?

Finally, he, too, closed his eyes.

Eric slept a dark, dreamless sleep until just before morning, when Jabbo appeared once again in a dream. He was in the smoky silver room, but he looked different. He still wore his fruit-smudged apron, but now a golden crown sat lopsided on his lumpy head.

He stared into the blue gem, then spoke. "It's whispering to King Jabbo again. Enemies are coming to take our power away! Rise, Hakoth-Mal! Let's find them first — even if we have to burn down the whole forest!"

Whoomf! He blew a huge flame from his mouth.

"Noooo!" Eric bolted up. It was morning. "Wake up, you guys! Wake up!"

Everyone roused themselves and rushed to him.

"Jabbo's even nuttier than before," said Eric. "He's calling himself king and says he'll destroy the whole forest to find us and stop us!"

Ortha gasped. "Then we have no time to lose. Let us be on our way. Hurry!"

The morning sun grew hotter and hotter as the group of nine traveled along the vine roads. Soon the cooling breezes died away. In the distance, a thick bank of low, dark clouds dripped down to earth in a ragged black fog.

And stretching out before them was a

single drooping bridge. On the far side, it clung to a black, leafless, ghostly trunk and ended there. All the trees beyond were bare, their branches black.

"The beginning of the Dark Lands," said Keeah.

"And the end of the wonderful vine roads," said Max.

"It looks like the end of the world," said Julie.

Ortha scanned the bridge. "We'll have to cross, then climb down to the ground."

"There's not much actual *ground* down there," said Eric, peering down. "It looks like a swamp — a deep one."

Galen nodded. "Here you see the ugliness of Sparr's domain. And yet we must enter into it." He stepped cautiously out onto the vines, pulling his cloak around him. "I weigh the most. If the bridge holds me up, it will support anyone."

"Master, be careful," said Max.

The bridge wobbled as Galen crept over it, carefully avoiding the ragged holes in its floor.

When he reached the other side, he called back, "Slowly now, and watch for torn vines!"

Twee and Woot crossed together. The others went one by one until only Eric and Keeah were left.

"Into the Dark Lands . . ." said Keeah.

She moved alone onto the bridge. When she reached the middle, Eric felt his heart flutter.

Something was wrong. He turned.

A dark blur streaked across the bridge, making it swing wildly from side to side.

"Stop!" said Keeah, turning. "Who's there —"

But Eric already knew.

The blur whooshed to his left, then

slowed and came down on the bridge in front of him.

It was the wingwolf he had seen in his dream, the Hakoth-Mal suited in red armor, its black wings whirring to a stop.

Eeeee! It shrieked.

"It's the ha-ha-not-funny guy!" yelled Neal.

"And that's not all," said Julie. "Look!"

Thwap-thwap-thwap!

Emerging from the clouds overhead was a great green lizard with large leathery wings.

"A groggle!" cried Ortha.

"With *him* on its back!" said Max.

It was Jabbo, grinning as he pulled hard on the lizard's reins. "Well done, Hakoth-Mal! You've hunted for Jabbo's enemies — and found them!"

The groggle grunted and hovered in the air above the bridge. Its heavy wings

flapped slowly, trapping Keeah where she stood.

Galen narrowed his eyes at the dragon. "Already he has become more like Sparr —"

"Jabbo is not Sparr!" the dragon yelled. "Jabbo is Jabbo, Ruler of Droon! King of . . . everything! And to prove it —"

Ha-rooomph! Jabbo blew a blast of flame from his mouth. It struck the bridge behind Keeah.

"No!" cried Eric, trying to get to her.

Fwip! Fwip! The wingwolf sprang in front of Eric, stopping him.

With fire on one side, and the wingwolf on the other, there was nowhere for Keeah to go.

"Help!" she screamed, as flames ripped across the bridge toward her.

Six

On the Last Bridge

Eric tried to get to Keeah, but the hunter's curved claws came flashing out — *shwee-shwee!*

"Oh, tough, aren't you?!" said Eric, leaping back. "Well, I'm a hero —"

He faked left, then right, and the wing-wolf followed his moves. "Ha!" Eric ducked under the creature's swinging claw and raced to Keeah in the middle of the bridge.

"Jabbo, call the creature off!" shouted Galen, edging out onto the bridge himself.

"But the Hakoth-Mal is so good at what he does!" said Jabbo, pulling his groggle up away from the leaping flames. "We make such a great team, there will be no stopping us!"

"Oh, we'll stop you!" cried Julie from the tree.

"Then we'll see who hunts who!" added Neal.

"Stop my enemies, wingwolf!" called Jabbo, lifting away. "Especially the ones with power. Steal their magic. Then join me to plan our *next* conquest!"

With that, Jabbo and his groggle lifted away, vanishing into the murky fog of the Dark Lands.

Without warning — *shwee-shwee!* — the wingwolf leaped at the kids.

Keeah jumped aside, and Eric crouched low, but the warrior's claws sliced at him.

Shwee — clack! Something fell to the bridge.

Eric looked down. His pocket was flapping open and the silver stone was sliding across the bridge.

"My dream stone!"

But even as he reached for it, the wingwolf lunged at Keeah, its claws outstretched.

"Leave her alone!" Eric shouted. Without thinking, he threw the stone as hard as he could at the warrior.

Flank! It struck the creature in the head, sending it staggering. The stone skittered across the floor of the bridge and fell through.

Eric made a grab for the stone, but it plummeted down through the air, twisting and turning as it fell.

The Hakoth-Mal leaped off the bridge and flew down to catch the stone. It grabbed it, howled once, then streaked away into the withered trees below.

In a moment, it was gone.

"Eric, come on!" cried Keeah, reaching for him.

Suddenly, the bridge snapped, sending Galen, Neal, and Julie leaping back to the far tree.

The flaming bridge sank under the two kids.

"Hold on!" called Ortha. With a mighty throw, she flung a vine to them.

Even as the bridge collapsed, Keeah grabbed the vine and pulled Eric up with her. "I've got you —"

Fwoosh! The flaming bridge fell into the swamp below, hissing and sputtering in the dark water.

Keeah and Eric swung to the ground nearby.

Julie was the first down from the tree and rushed to them. "Are you guys all right?"

Keeah nodded. "I am. Eric, what about you?"

He frowned as Keeah helped him up. "I'm okay, but, man! I was supposed to save you. In my dream I was the hero. Instead, *you* saved *me,* and I lost the stone!"

"But why did the Hakoth-Mal steal it from you?" asked Woot, scampering over to the children.

"It's magic, of course," said Twee. "I've always thought so. It's so shiny."

Eric remembered the voice in his dream and how the mysterious hand had given him the stone.

"Anyway," he said, "I want it back."

"We'll get it back," said Keeah. "I promise —"

"Hush, a moment," said Galen, peering into the distance. "I hear . . . I hear . . ."

"Jabbo coming back?" asked Neal.

"The Faraway?" asked Eric.

Ortha shook her head. "No . . . look there."

At that moment, a strange blue light flashed through the high trees and flitted down to them, singing, "Galennn! Galennnnn!"

"Flink," cried Max, jumping up and down. "It's Flink! With a message for my master."

The light seemed to seek out the wizard from among them and spun over his head swiftly. It spoke to him in strange musical tones.

"Ah," said Galen finally. "It seems I must go help King Zello and Queen Relna.

But I promise to return as soon as I can. You must go on."

The children looked around. The ground was swampy and the water in it foul-smelling and black.

"If you ask me," said Neal, "I think we pretty much need you, too. Let's face it, the Dark Lands are not exactly the fun and games capital of Droon."

The wizard smiled. "And yet, there is much you can do on your own. I am needed elsewhere. You must continue without me."

"Are my parents in danger?" asked Keeah.

There was a flash in the old man's eyes that meant the danger was very real.

"I shall be there before it comes to that. But what you do here may be even more important. Max, stay with our princess and our friends."

The spider troll nodded firmly. "I will stick to them like my own sticky silk!"

"That's the fellow," said Galen. "I must go now. Flink, lead the way."

Galen waved good-bye, then headed south into the woods, following the sparkling blue light.

Moments later, he was gone.

"And now, we must go on," said Ortha, scanning the swamp that lay before them.

The vast marshes were studded with the cracked stumps of fallen trees. Thin, twisted branches thrust up from the murky water like pale, bony hands.

"Go on," said Eric. "But how?"

"We sure ran out of climbing trees," said Neal.

"And the water is too shallow for a boat," said Julie, "and a little too deep to walk through."

"I have an idea!" said Woot. She huddled with Twee for a second. They both laughed, then began to gather fallen sticks and branches.

"What are you up to?" said Ortha.

"Just you wait," said Twee. "You'll see!"

For the next five minutes, the two monkeys busied themselves with the branches. Finally, they finished.

"What have you made?" asked Keeah.

Twee showed them. "I took the longest branches and bent them into U-shapes."

"And I wove some stout green branches into the middles," said Woot.

Twee handed several of the U-shaped branches to Keeah and Neal. "Try them on!"

Neal laughed. "Are you expecting a change in the weather? These look like . . . snowshoes!"

"Oh, I see. They are swamp shoes!" said Max, slipping on four pairs of his own.

"With these, we can walk right across the thick water!"

"Which we must do at once," said Ortha, taking command. "Come now, everyone. Jabbo grows stronger by the minute. *O — lee — lee! O — lee — lee!*"

The monkey queen's call echoed into the blackened forest, and the small band — smaller now without Galen — set off once more.

Seven

The Silent Stones Speak

The sun's light was choked by a thick brown haze as the eight friends entered the Dark Lands.

Splog! Kloosh! Plurp!

Tree roots stretched like fingers out over the swamp, making their passage across the water slow and dangerous.

"Steady there!" said Max as they squashed across the surface of the water.

"I can't even see two steps ahead," said Eric.

"I can't breathe!" said Neal. "The air is as thick as a blanket on my nose. A stinky blanket!"

Julie tried to wave away the heavy air. "From a beautiful green forest to this? Very yucky."

"Quite right," said Ortha. "If nothing else, this shows you the power of evil —"

Eeeeee! A piercing, eerie sound came from somewhere in the smoky air above.

"Okay, I'm scared," said Neal. "That wingy dude is officially creeping me out."

Eric swatted the smoky air. "Creepy or not, I can't wait to see him again . . . and get my stone back."

"We'll find your stone," said Keeah. "I have a feeling we'll see that creature again very soon."

"When we do," said Julie, "you'll grab your dream stone. And boot that wolf out of here."

Eric smiled at his friends. "Thanks, guys."

But he wondered if it would really be that easy. If Jabbo kept growing in power, thanks to Sparr's gem, maybe the little pie maker and the wingwolf really *could* conquer Droon.

One hour, two hours, they slogged their way across the black swamp. Finally, it gave way to hard, dry land once more. And in the middle of the barren wood, the forest was strangely green again.

Ortha looked up. The sky was still dark, the air brown and thick. "Something, not the land and the rain and the sun, keeps these trees growing — oh!"

A sudden wind wafted across them.

And there, just beyond a bank of twisted underbrush was what looked like a wall of giant stones, now tumbled to the ground.

Twee tugged the sleeve of Keeah's tunic and looked up at her, his eyes huge with wonder.

"Princess," he whispered. "I think we have found it. The lost temple of the old legends!"

Climbing over the stones, the small band came into a large clearing. There, they saw the remains of once-tall towers, now no more than crumbled stones, ruined walls, fallen balconies, and stairs that circled high, leading nowhere.

But most remarkable of all was that even in the smoky light, the stones, broken and crumbled as they were, shone like silver.

Eric shivered. "This is where I saw Jabbo in my dream. And this is where my stone came from."

Ortha cast her eyes solemnly around. "Time has not been kind to this place."

"It is old," said Max softly. "So old, it doesn't even appear on Galen's map."

As they passed deeper into the ruins

they spied the great central tower of the temple in the distance. Of all the buildings, it alone seemed unhurt by time. Layer upon layer of silvery stone pushed it skyward.

Behind it grew a giant tree, thicker than any other in the forest. Its upper limbs were lost in the fog above.

"It must have taken thousands of people to build this place," said Julie.

Twee giggled softly. "The legend says that the temple is the work of a giant bird who brought the stones one by one in his great curved beak."

"Some say the temple was built by giants!" said Woot. "Or else, who could climb that high?"

"And how do *you* think the temple came to be?" asked Keeah.

"Simple!" said Twee. "It made itself!"

The children wanted to laugh, but the

more they explored the ruins, the more they began to think that perhaps the temple *had* made itself.

Or *grown* itself.

For here and there the jungle and the temple had become one. There were small trees growing up from the stones, making the structure itself seem in some magical way . . . like a living thing.

"If Jabbo is here," said Julie, "I wonder if the Eye of the Viper brought him here."

"It's really just a pile of stones," added Neal.

"And yet, there's something more here," said Keeah, her eyes wandering among the shapes of the stones.

"I'm picking it up, too," said Eric. "But I can't tell what — whoa!"

When they entered the main courtyard they stopped.

The giant tree they had seen earlier did not grow from behind the great temple spire — it grew *from* the temple.

It was gigantic, towering over the ruins, and seeming to tower over all of Droon!

"I've never seen a tree so — big!" Julie exclaimed. "The trunk must be a hundred feet around. It's growing right out of the temple!"

The tree's massive trunk and roots seemed draped over the stones as if a thick gray liquid had been poured from the sky and had hardened in place, snaking down between the stones to the black earth below.

Above, the limbs of the tree twisted up in such number that someone might climb from the very bottom all the way to the top of the forest.

"Now that's what I call a climbing tree,"

said Neal. "It's even better than your apple trees back home, Eric. And a whole lot taller!"

On the front of the temple where one might have expected a door, there was instead a large face carved from several blocks of stone. It was the face of a woman, and it bore a strange smile.

Eric felt his heart flutter again. The face's eyes were closed as if it were asleep. As if it might be . . . dreaming.

He longed, suddenly, to hear the voice in his dream again.

The faraway voice.

"It's so beautiful here," said Julie. "So quiet."

"Too quiet," said Max with a scowl. "But it's not as if no one is here. It's more as if someone, or something, is here, but holding its breath."

Neal's eyes widened. "It's holding mine,

too. This place is giving me the major spooks —"

Eeeee! A shrill cry pierced the air.

Eric whirled around. "The Hakoth-Mal. Up there. Near the base of the spire! Give me back my stone, you creepy thing!"

A second later, the creature streaked down from the temple and landed on the ground. In a flash — *klish-ang!* — its claws were out.

"Children, stay back," cried Ortha. Grabbing a stick, she leaped to the top of a tumbled stone. "There's a time for peace, and a time to fight back! Hee-yah!"

The monkey queen sprang at the creature, making her own green blur in the air. The wolf tripped before it had a chance to swing its claws.

"Find Jabbo! Take Sparr's gem from him!" Ortha said, driving the wingwolf off with her stick — *clack! clonk! clang!*

Woot and Twee followed her, swatting the creature with their own sticks, leaping away into the jungle after their queen.

"Ortha, wait! We'll help you!" Keeah called.

But Max held her arm. "No, Princess, look — the stone face — it's moving!"

As the children stood in front of it — *vrrrrt!* — the stones trembled and suddenly flew aside.

Eric tried to brace himself. "Wait . . . no!"

He fell forward into the darkness.

Neal, Julie, Max, and Keeah tumbled after him — sliding, sliding, sliding — until they slammed down on a cold stone floor.

And there he was, sitting on a magnificent jeweled throne.

Jabbo the dragon.

Jabbo the powerful.

Jabbo the king.

Eight

The Everything King?

The room was different from Eric's dream. It wasn't so dim.

Torch light glinted against the silvery walls. Long tapestries hung from the ceiling. And the big throne was set high against the back wall of the room.

But Jabbo had changed even more.

Gone was the smudged apron with the fruit stains. Now he wore a long red cape trimmed in gold, giant boots studded with silver buttons, and an even larger gold crown on his knobby head.

But most important, Jabbo had a big sword.

In the handle was the blue gem, glowing fiercely.

"So, you survived Jabbo's little fire, did you?" the dragon asked.

No one said a word. They were all staring at the sword.

"Yes, the Eye of the Viper," said the dragon, rising from his throne. "Jabbo put it in the sword, because soon there will be a big old battle in Droon. Jabbo against all of you!" *Swish-swish!*

"The Eye of the Viper is dangerous," said Keeah. "Not even Galen knows its full power. You need to give it up. You can't control it."

Jabbo smiled. "But I'm dressed to take over."

"Ha!" said Neal. "It looks like you already did take over — the Halloween costume store!"

"Silence!" cried Jabbo. "You must give the new king of Droon your respect! Or I shall use the Eye on you!"

He wagged his sword at them.

Eric looked around. The walls to the right and left were the same silver as his dream stone. But the back wall of the room was curved and gray. It was the trunk of the great tree.

A liquid was *drip-drip-dripping* down from the branches above and filling a small fountain near where Jabbo had set his throne.

The water — if it was water — seemed to gleam and flash even in the torchlight.

"We know some of the words the Eye is telling you," said Keeah. "They do pretty bad things. The Hakoth-Mal serve Lord

Sparr . . . not you. It is Sparr who holds the Eye's twin — the other jewel."

"Humph!" Jabbo snarled. "For years, all I did was take flour, water, salt, butter, roll it out, add fruit, bake until golden brown. Well, I don't want to be a simple pie maker anymore. I want to be — the big pie!"

He whirled on his heels, grabbed a golden goblet from the throne, dipped it into the fountain, and drank.

When he did, he suddenly began to glow as silver as the walls of the room. He twitched. He jerked. "Oh! Another dream going out! Eeeek! Arrgh! Wooo! And Jabbo takes over another dream in Droon!"

He slumped back into his throne.

Keeah gasped, then nudged Eric. "The water? Is that how Jabbo's getting into our dreams?"

Eric looked down. Cracks in the floor

stones told him there was another room below them.

"Maybe," he whispered. "We need to get down there somehow. Down to the roots."

"If only Ortha was here," said Keeah. "She could help us get down there."

Neal raised his hand. "Um, Jabbo, can I ask why your cape is so long?"

The dragon grinned. "You'll find out soon enough why my cape is so long. It all has to do with Jabbo's gem —"

Julie shook her head. "But it's Sparr's gem. The Hakoth-Mal hunts down *his* enemies. What happens if Sparr comes back? You'll be his enemy, too."

A look of fear crossed the little dragon's face. Then he trembled. "You're trying to trick Jabbo — oh! No, no! When I get angry — it happens!"

"What happens?" asked Eric.

Suddenly, the jewel began to glow in the sword. In an instant, blue light flashed up Jabbo's hand and covered him completely. "This," he cried out, "this — is why my cape is so long — ohhhhh!"

All at once, the little dragon began to grow. His head and body grew to twice their size. The spikes on his back became long and sharp. And his jaws, opening wide, suddenly shot out a powerful stream of fire. *Ka-whooom!*

"Yikes!" cried Max. "Let's get out of here!"

"Way ahead of you!" shouted Julie. "Exit, this way!" She jumped to a round opening in the wall and into a narrow passage leading up.

Neal and Max raced after her.

Eric glanced through the cracks in the

floor at the room below, but Keeah pulled him with her. "Come on!"

Whoom! Whoo-hoom! Jabbo's blasts of fire grew as he himself grew. He bounded up the passage after the children, his fire spraying them as he chased them up and out of the temple.

"Over here!" Keeah shouted, leaping behind a tumbled wall with Eric. Julie jumped over, landing right next to them.

Neal and Max skittered across the clearing inches ahead of Jabbo, but Neal tripped. When he did, the last few monkey biscuits fell out of his pocket and scattered across the ground.

Jabbo, now huge and angry, sent a burst of fire at the tumbling biscuits — *whoomf!*

The little squares flamed and turned black, filling the air with the smell of burned dough.

"My biscuits!" Neal yelled, even as Julie

and Max dragged him to safety behind the wall.

The giant dragon stopped thrashing around. He lowered the sword to his side and stared at the tiny black squares smoking on the ground.

"Biscuits?" he asked softly. "Burned to a crisp?"

"Bangledorn monkey biscuits," said Neal peeking out from behind the wall. "I was saving them. . . ."

The dragon groaned. "Jabbo — Jabbo! What have you done?! You never burn things!"

Instantly, the blue glow vanished into the sword. Then, right before their eyes, Jabbo began to shrink. The spikes down his back softened to little nubs. His fire-breathing jaws shortened to a stubby green snout.

In moments, Jabbo was his old, small

size again, huddled in the pile of his long capes.

Trembling, he began to sniffle.

Max tugged Keeah's sleeve. "Is this a trick? Or is Jabbo really . . . crying?"

Cautiously, Keeah stepped out from behind the wall. "Jabbo, are you all right?"

"I never burn things!" said the little dragon, his chest heaving. "I never would have done any of this, if it hadn't been for this silly jewel —"

Clank! He tossed the sword to the ground. "All I really want in Droon is . . . a good oven."

Julie blinked, then glanced at Keeah and Eric. "An oven? To bake things in?"

"Yes!" said Jabbo, lifting his face up. "One that doesn't overbake the bottoms of my pies. One that will give me a nice, flaky crust —" His eyes grew large. "It's all in the crust, you know. Jabbo dreams of flaky crusts. Well, he used to dream, before all of this. And good fruit. Ripe berries —"

"Gizzleberries are the best!" said Max, stepping slowly over to the little dragon.

"Gizzleberries?" asked the pie maker, wiping his scaly cheeks. "Jabbo never heard of those."

"They're in season now in Droon," said Max. "Purple and fat and juicy!"

"Ohhh! They sound wonderful!" said Jabbo, letting his crown slip off and clatter to the ground. "It's too much! Stealing all these silly dreams, and yes — nightmares, too! It brought me so much power! And at first, I thought being supreme king of everything would be fun. But all I really want is to bake. . . ."

"You don't have to take over Droon for that," said Eric.

Jabbo's eyes brightened. "No, I don't, do I?"

"Not at all," said Keeah. "And you won't need the gem, either." She picked up the sword. With one quick move, she popped the gem out of the handle.

Jabbo looked up. "Good. I won't hear that evil voice whispering in my ear anymore."

"Sparr's voice, no doubt," said Max. He scurried over, taking a small gold box from a pouch on his belt, and clicked it open.

Keeah placed the gem in the box and snapped the lid shut. "Let Sparr talk to himself in there!"

Julie grinned. "That's that, then —"

"Except for one thing," said Jabbo, removing his old smudged apron from a pocket in his cape and tying it on. "We still have *him* to worry about!"

He pointed up into the branches of the huge tree. There, high above them all, was a shape.

The shape of an armed warrior with wings.

Eeeeee! It shrieked at them, holding up a clawed hand. In it was a small round stone.

"He must have outwitted Ortha," said Keeah.

"Oh, yeah?" Eric shouted. "Well, this time, things will be different. This time — the hunter becomes the hunted! Get ready, wolfy, because we're coming after you!"

Nine

Battle in the Branches

Eeeee! The wingwolf's cry echoed over the temple as if the air were being ripped in half.

"I'll get you!" said Eric, bounding up the tree.

Julie, Neal, Keeah, and Max all grabbed thick sticks and shot up right behind him.

The creature sprang from branch to branch as the children charged up. It flashed its clawed hands across the air, shrieking again.

"If only we could fly like him," said Julie, "then it would be even."

"We'll still beat him," said Neal. "Well, we'd better!"

As Eric clambered up from one branch to another, he heard the dream voice again, but this time it wasn't in his head. It seemed to come from somewhere outside him.

Somewhere very close.

The one who strikes the wolf at noon, shall earn a secret wish in Droon.

Eric looked up through the haze. The sun was just behind the clouds. It was nearly noon.

"I'll do it," he whispered. "I'll be the hero!"

But even as he pulled himself up, the wingwolf dived at him. The glittering flash of its claws sent Eric reeling back against the thick trunk.

The creature slashed the bark.

Ahhhh! came a whispered cry. *Eric! Eric!*

"Oh, my gosh!" he gasped. "The tree —"

"Eric, watch out!" cried Keeah, pulling herself to a large branch below him.

The wingwolf's black wings hummed as it dived again. *Eeeee!*

"We'll get him from below!" said Keeah.

"And I'll get him from here!" said Neal, creeping along the branch above, his stick ready.

Keeah and Julie darted out to the end of a thick branch, bounced on it once, twice, three times, then leaped up next to Eric.

The creature swiveled around to them. Its wolvish eyes burned like flame.

"Down, boy!" cried Neal. "Leave them alone!" He whacked his stick across the wolf's back — *clang-ang-ang!* Neal's arm quivered. "M-m-man! Even his-s-s armor-r-r has armor!"

"He's coming again!" shouted Max. He scrambled up the trunk and let loose a spray of sticky spider silk at the creature.

Swish! Swish! The wingwolf slashed the silken trap to nothing.

"He broke right through," said Neal. "Abandon ship! I mean, abandon tree —"

Suddenly, there was a swift cracking sound, and — *whoosh!* — a single brown nut came crashing up through the leaves and smacked the wingwolf in the head.

"*Gaaaakkkk!*" The creature staggered.

Neal blinked. "Where did that nut come from?"

The answer was a call from below.

"*O — lee — lee! O — lee — lee!*"

"What‽" said Julie. "Could it be‽ It's Ortha!"

"This is the hour of the Bangledorn monkeys!" echoed the familiar voice. "Goodbye, Wingwolf! This is when we take our forest back! Monkeys, help our friends!"

Eric punched the air. "Yes! Reinforcements!"

In a flash, the tree was alive with hundreds of green shapes. Twee and Woot scampered up, carrying a bundle of woven vines between them.

Woot's red-sashed friends were tossing up the nuts, and Twee's purple-scarfed friends were batting them at the wingwolf with their sticks. All the monkeys were working together.

Bonk! Clonk! "Gaaaakkkk!"

"Hey, it looks like baseball's now the official game of Bangledorn Forest!" said Julie.

"Blast some home runs, you guys," said Eric.

And they did. *Crack! Whoosh! Blonk!*

The wingwolf was pummeled with nut after flying nut. It didn't know which way to turn.

"We've been practicing!" squealed one monkey. "Thank you, Neal!"

"And now for the winning play!" said Twee. He and Woot scampered up to the highest branches. They unrolled a giant net made of vines.

"Everyone take hold!" said Ortha. "Ready? One, two, three, now —"

With Neal, Julie, and Keeah on one side, and Twee, Woot, and Max on the other, they threw the viney net. As the wingwolf whirred its wings to fly up — *flump!* — it was caught.

Tugging the ends of the net, the monkeys closed it tightly around the creature.

The creature made another high-pitched gargling noise — "*gaaaakkkk!*" — and writhed and wiggled in its trap of vines.

Max spun a thick web of spider silk and wove it around the vine net. "Just to be sure!" he said.

Eric glared at the wingwolf, its eyes still burning brightly. "Now, give me that stone!"

He forced the creature's claws open, took his silvery dream stone back, and clasped it in his own hand once more.

"Yes! It's mine again!" Laughing, Eric turned to his friends. "It's just like you guys said —"

He didn't finish. Snarling and shrieking, the wingwolf thrust out its claws again. *Shwee* —

The claw flew past Eric and swiped Julie's hand. "Oww!" she said.

The scratch turned red instantly.

"I'll get him!" said Eric. "I'll *strike the wolf at noon*!"

But the creature slashed at him next, pushing him off balance. In an instant, Julie struck the Hakoth-Mal with her stick. The wolf howled and went silent.

Eric gasped. As he clutched for a limb to hold him, his eyes glanced up.

It was brightest right overhead.

It was the very moment of noon.

"Julie!" he said, slipping backward. "It's not me . . . it's . . . *you*!"

That was the last thing he said.

Before he fell off the tree.

Ten

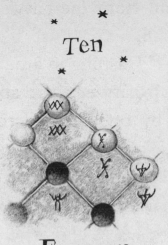

Faraway

"Eric!" cried Keeah.

He tried to grasp branches as he fell, but he plummeted too quickly.

Then, at the very instant he thought he would be thrown against the temple stones, he heard that voice again. That faraway voice.

Eric . . .

A sudden wind, like a warm breath,

blew upward from the silver temple and slowed his fall.

"What —" Gasping in amazement, Eric floated down between the spire's stones, which one by one seemed to part as he fell.

He landed gently on his feet in a giant stone room at the very bottom level of the temple.

The room was filled with the music of water, gurgling down to a pool at the roots of the giant tree.

Welcome . . .

The word echoed for what seemed like hours.

"The tree," he whispered finally. "This is where the dreams come from. The voice is here . . . but . . . whose voice . . . is it?"

He stepped closer, then stopped.

Even in the dim light, he saw the answer.

Clutched between the thick roots, entwined with them, as if the roots themselves were the fingers of a giant hand, was a long glass box.

Eric felt his heart slow.

Lying in the box was the figure of a woman. She wore a long white gown and a golden crown upon her head. Her face was old and pale, but magically seemed as fresh as the apple blossoms on the trees in his yard.

Somehow Eric knew who it was.

It was her, the mother of Galen and Urik. The mother of Lord Sparr, too. The mother who had been lost so long ago. He had found her.

"Zara," he said. Her name sounded in the room like a feather falling softly to the ground.

For five centuries I have dreamed of Droon.

Her voice swam in his head like a song

he knew he had never heard, but which sounded strangely familiar.

"You send dreams to lots of people," he said. "Even to me and my friends. Why?"

So that the wonder of Droon will not die.

"But why to me?" he said. "I goof up. I make all kinds of mistakes. Dumb mistakes. I'm not that special. I'm just . . . me."

To Eric, the sound that followed was like a song or a laugh or both.

Long ago you could have hidden from our struggles. Closed the door to Droon.

He shook his head. "I couldn't do that. Ever."

And that is why you are . . . one of us.

His heart quickened. "But what does that mean?"

Look around!

Eric looked up at the high walls of the

room. On every one, shining in the light of the pool, were small round stones just like his. They, too, were carved with symbols — names — in the old language of Droon. Thin glistening lines connected one stone to another to another in a giant web.

"My stone is like these. Who are they?"

Wizards of Droon.

Eric went to the wall and peered closely at the stones. He believed he saw Galen's name and Urik's. Not far away were Queen Relna's name and Keeah's, too.

Near Keeah's was an empty place, waiting for a stone to fill it.

Go ahead. . . . and behold your future . . .

As the music of the water wove around him, Eric held the stone up between his thumb and first finger. Trembling as he reached, he placed it in the vacant spot on the wall.

The stone clicked into place. When it did, a sudden silvery light flooded out from the crystal tomb and into his eyes.

"Whoa!" he gasped, stumbling back from the wall as he was struck with a vision of the future.

What he saw was a vast desert at night. Moonbeams reflected off one rolling dune after another.

And there they were, the four of them, Julie, Neal, Keeah, and him. They rode four pilkas side by side at the head of a long twisting caravan.

Glistening on the horizon far, far in the distance stood a fabulous city of light.

Eric smiled. "It looks like a long journey."

How long he watched the four of them, if it were hours, or if it was only an instant, Eric couldn't tell. But when the vision faded, he was left standing in the room.

"That was awesome," he whispered.

"It was us. Together. Just like I hope it will always be."

Your road will not be easy, Eric. Among the good days, dark times will come. For you. For Keeah. For Julie and Neal, too. The darkest of all your lives.

He breathed in. "Will we be okay?"

That is a question you yourselves will answer. Help one another. Help Julie. She has a power now, and perhaps more than one. Together, you will —

The voice stopped. The light began to dim.

"Zara? What will happen?" asked Eric, straining to hear her voice again. "Zara, tell me. . . ."

A stone shifted in the wall behind him. He turned.

"Ooof! Owww! Yikes! Hey, Eric — !"

It was Neal, groaning as he tumbled into the chamber from the room above.

Keeah and Julie crashed to the floor behind him.

"Eric!" said Keeah, jumping over to him. "Are you all right? We saw you fall and then — oh! Oh, my gosh! Oh!"

They all stared at the glass box.

"It's Zara," said Eric softly, noticing for the first time that it no longer hurt to say her name.

"What just happened here?" said Neal.

Eric smiled at his friends, especially Julie. Her hand was bandaged by leaves wound with Max's spider silk. "I just had a vision," he said. "I learned about all of us — about our future."

Just then, they heard a great cheer go up from the monkeys outside, and the name Galen was shouted over and over.

A moment later, the tall, blue-robed wizard came down the shaft and into the room.

"I have come with some news of Sala-mandra," Galen said.

Then he stopped and stared.

No one spoke as he approached the glass tomb. Tears rolled down his weathered cheeks and were lost in his white beard.

"Your mother," whispered Eric. "It was her all the time, sending us dreams from this tree."

"The Faraway," said Julie.

The old wizard nodded his head slowly. "And you have found her. At last . . . at last! Her love of Droon grows from where her body rests. She will never be lost again."

Galen stood silently for a moment, then looked up at his friends. "Come. Let us go now. Much happens in Droon that requires us."

Eric longed to hear more of Zara's

words, but found that along with the silver light her voice had already faded. But it was okay. He was with his friends. That was what really mattered.

Silently, reverently, they all stepped away from the tomb.

When they climbed out of the temple, Ortha and the monkeys were jumping up and down.

"The sun. Look. It's back!" cried Twee.

It was true. The dark brown haze had rolled back completely and sunlight shone through the branches of the tree onto the silver stones of the temple.

"And look there," said Ortha.

The wingwolf lay in its vine trap, frozen to solid stone.

"He's just a lump of rock!" said Neal.

"And so he will be as long as the sun of Droon shines on him," said Galen.

"Which will be forever, if Woot and I

have anything to say about it!" added Twee.

"Woo-hoo!" Julie slapped high fives with Keeah and Neal, and again with Max and Eric.

"Our victory today has driven back the Dark Lands!" said Galen, smiling. "We have struck a blow against all the forces of evil in Droon. Today has been good. But even as we win here, wicked Salamandra stirs up trouble in the west!"

"My mother and father need me," said Keeah.

"And we shall go," said Galen. "But first, a little unfinished business — Max!"

The spider troll brought Jabbo forward.

The little dragon kept his eyes down. "Jabbo made much trouble for Droon. But he still bakes the best pies. Shall he bake a gizzleberry pie for the great wizard?"

Galen frowned at the little dragon,

then, with Ortha by his side, his expression softened.

"Yes, perhaps. And I know just the place for that. Firefrog Mountain. You can bake, and we can keep an eye on you."

The kids remembered Firefrog Mountain. It was an island far across Droon, inhabited by friendly watchers called firefrogs.

"We shall bring him there," said Ortha.

Woot saluted. "And Twee and I will help!"

"Now we must begin our journey back," said Galen. "And so must you, children. Look!"

Above the high tree, shining like a rainbow in the new, golden sunlight, were the magic stairs to the Upper World.

"I guess it's that time again," said Neal.

As the three friends started for the tree, Eric glanced once more upon the temple.

"This really is a special place," he said.

"And it shall be honored," said Ortha solemnly. "Now that all of our forest is in sunlight again, we shall rebuild the temple of Zara."

"Sparr had better not set foot here again," said Galen. "Yet, if I know him, he will try. He will try."

While Galen and Ortha prepared to leave the forest, Keeah hugged her friends. "Good-bye, Eric, Neal. And Julie, take care of that cut."

"I will," she said. "It doesn't even hurt."

Eric frowned for a moment, wondering what would happen now, and what Julie's *secret wish* was. Then he remembered the vision of the four friends. They would be together for a long time to come. Whatever happened, it would be okay.

"Good-bye, Keeah," said Neal. "At least for now. We probably won't stay away too long."

"I hope not!" she said.

Eric smiled and nodded at the temple. "I'm sure our dreams will call us back soon."

As Ortha, Galen, Max, Keeah, and the monkeys hurried away to their new adventures, the three friends climbed up the great tree toward the stairs.

When they poked their heads through the top branches, they glimpsed again the sunlit sea of trees swaying all the way to the horizon.

Julie took a deep breath. "Guys?" she said.

"Yeah?" said Eric.

"Do you think it will always be like this?"

Neal grinned. "I hope so. I love the adventure. The excitement. The monkey baseball! Eric?"

Eric glanced at the stairs shimmering

above them, then smiled. "I think it'll just keep getting better. And the best part is, it's no dream. This is for real."

Neal whooped. "I like the sound of that! Come on. After a quick round of your dad's waffles, we're going to build some tree houses!"

Laughing, Julie turned to the stairs. Then, in a blur of speed, she flew straight up in the air. As if she had wings.

"Oh, my gosh!" she gasped at the top of the stairs. "I always wanted to fly!"

Eric and Neal stared at each other, gulped, then raced up the stairs after her.